Francine

Grandma Thora

Mum

Binky

The Brain

Mr Ratburn

£5.99

Written by Lynne Gibbs
Illustrated by Chris Russell/Specs Art
Designed by Jason Bazini

©1999 Marc Brown.
All characters and underlying materials (including artwork) copyrighted by Marc Brown.
"Arthur", "D.W." and all of the Arthur characters are trademarks of Marc Brown.

Published by Grandreams Limited
435-437 Edgware Road
Little Venice, London W2 1TH

Printed in Belgium

The Official Annual

Contents

Hi, everyone !

My name is Arthur – and I'd like to welcome you to my very first Arthur Annual! Inside, you can read all about the exciting adventures I have with my friends and family. There are puzzles for you to do, a board game to play – and even a game to make! So have hours and hours of fun!
Big kisses and hugs,

Love, Arthur

6

"I hope you like this photograph of me, my friends and family," says Arthur. "Below you'll find everyone's name, too."

Back row: Grandma Thora, Mum (holding Baby Kate), Dad, D.W.

Middle row: The Brain, Buster, Binky, Francine, Prunella, and my teacher, Mr. Ratburn.

Front row: Arthur and his puppy, Pal.

Lemonade, Anyone?

It was a very hot day, so Grandma Thora made lemonade to help keep everyone cool.
"It's too hot to cook anything for tea," sighed Arthur's mum, standing in front of a big fan.

Dad had an idea. "If you two hurry and change into your swimsuits, I'll prepare a nice surprise for everyone!" he said.
Arthur and D.W. rushed out of the room.

While Mum carried a covered tray into the garden, Dad went to fetch something from his shed.
"I won't be long!" called Dad, as he banged and crashed around.

After playing in their rooms for a while, Arthur and D.W. came back into the kitchen, where Grandma Thora was busy making more jugs of lemonade. "Take these outside, children," she smiled, "and try not to spill any, won't you?"

"Oh, I'm ever so careful," smiled Arthur, carrying a jug.

But all of a sudden, he tripped on a clump of earth and spilt his jug of lemonade – all over poor D.W.!

Luckily, Grandma Thora had more lemonade – and D.W. had another swimming costume to wear! "I wonder what Dad's surprise is?" said D.W., as she and Arthur balanced their lemonade.

"Fire! Fire!" cried Arthur, pointing to smoke rising above a big bush at the far end of the garden.

"What shall we do?" gasped D.W.

10

Hardly hesitating, Arthur ran over to the bush - and threw his jug of lemonade over the top! Then D.W. did the same!

On the other side of the bush, Mum, Dad and Baby Kate gasped as lemonade splashed all over them!

11

"I-I thought there was a fire," gasped Arthur, as he and D.W. ran round to the other side of the bush.

"I was just preparing a barbeque," sighed Dad, staring at the wet, hissing coals.

"More lemonade, anyone?" asked Grandma Thora, who had missed all the excitement.

"No, I think I've had quite enough for one day," said Dad.

Everyone looked at each other – and burst out laughing!

Which Path?

Which path should Arthur take through the flowerbeds to reach the big bush, where Dad is waiting for him?

Turn to page 60 if you need help finding the right path!

Spot the Changes

When Arthur and D.W. saw smoke, they thought there
was a fire! Throwing their jugs of lemonade over a bush,
they soaked Mum, Dad and poor Baby Kate! Can you see
how these two pictures are different in twelve ways?

Turn to page 60 if you need help spotting the changes!

Buried Treasure!

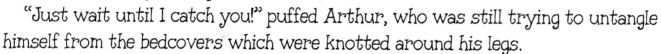

"Come back here!" laughed Arthur, as his mischievous puppy ran round and round the bedroom. But Pal wanted to play. Before Arthur could stop him, Pal tugged Arthur's slipper off his foot and raced underneath the bed! Arthur tried to follow, but he just wasn't quite quick enough!

Still holding the slipper firmly between his teeth, Pal scrambled out the other side, jumped over Arthur's train set, between the legs of a chair – and through the open bedroom door!

"Just wait until I catch you!" puffed Arthur, who was still trying to untangle himself from the bedcovers which were knotted around his legs.

After getting dressed, Arthur went downstairs to search for Pal. Going into the kitchen, he looked under the table, inside the kitchen cupboards and even in the rubbish bin! But Pal wasn't in any of those places.

When Arthur heard a strange scraping sound coming from the living room, his heart almost missed a beat.

"Oh Pal, please don't say you've found Grandma Thora's shopping again!" he gasped.

Peering behind an armchair, Arthur found his puppy trying to 'bury' things under a pile of torn newspapers. Pal had chewed Grandma Thora's favourite hat, Dad's wallet, D.W.'s book and Baby Kate's rattle!

"You're in big trouble now, naughty puppy!" whispered Arthur.

Arthur's mum didn't look at all happy when she saw what Pal had done. Pointing towards the garden, she said just one word, "OUTSIDE!"

Pal didn't need telling twice. Keeping his eyes to the ground, the puppy dodged between Arthur's legs and raced into the garden.

A little later, when she thought the puppy had learned his lesson, Mum told Arthur to fetch Pal inside.

But the puppy was having far too much fun. Holding a chewed flowerpot between his teeth, Pal raced in and out of Dad's flowerbeds, scattering flowers everywhere!

"We'll catch him!" called Arthur, as he and D.W. chased Pal around the garden. But the faster Arthur and D.W. ran, the faster Pal ran, turfing up clumps of grass as he went!

"Oh no!" cried Arthur's mum as Pal jumped on to her basket of clean washing, leaving muddy paw prints behind.

Dashing through the washing-line, Pal pulled down a clean sheet. With the sheet covering his head, the puppy couldn't see where he was going – and ran straight into the garden pond!

SPLASH! It was difficult to tell who was the most surprised – Pal, or the frogs who leaped out of the water!

Arthur's dad ordered Pal to his kennel. The bedraggled puppy climbed out of the pond, shook his wet fur over everyone, then sadly walked into his little home.

While Dad picked up the broken flowerpots and flowers, Arthur and D.W. jumped up and down on the clumps of turf that Pal had pulled out of the ground.

Suddenly, something bright and shiny caught Arthur's eye. Bending down, he raked through the loose earth.

"It's buried treasure!" gasped D.W. as Arthur held up his find.

"Clever Arthur! You've found my gold locket and chain!" laughed Grandma, coming over to see what all the excitement was about.

As everyone gathered round, Grandma Thora explained that she had lost the locket a long, long time ago.

"If it hadn't been for Pal digging up the lawn, I would never have found it!" chuckled Arthur.

"Mmm, I suppose you're right," grinned Dad.

"Who's a good boy, then!" said Grandma Thora, as she and the rest of the family made a big fuss of Pal.

Pal didn't quite understand what he had done, but he liked being hugged and given his favourite doggie chocolate drops!

HIDDEN

20

TREASURES

Arthur's playful puppy has hidden lots of things in the garden. As you find the objects drawn around the page hidden in the big picture, tick the circle next to each object. You can check the answers on page 60.

21

Matching Sweeties

Can you help Arthur, Binky and Buster to pair-up the sweets which are exactly the same? Look carefully at the wrappers and the shapes!

Turn to page 60 if you need help matching the sweeties!

Too Many Sweets!

Arthur and his friends listened as Mr. Ratburn told a story about a monkey who lost everything because he was so greedy.

"I thought greedy people got more, not less," said Binky.

"Not always," smiled their teacher. "Let me show you." Mr. Ratburn told Arthur he could keep all the marbles he managed to take out of a jar, using just one hand.

"Look, I've got four marbles!" laughed Arthur.

Then Binky tried to take a huge handful of marbles from the jar.

"My hand's stuck!" gasped Binky. He had to let go of all the marbles before he could free his hand. "Greedy Binky has lost all his marbles!" said the class.

Next day, Arthur entered a competition at his local supermarket - and correctly guessed how many sweets were inside a jar.

As his prize, Arthur and two friends were allowed two minutes to take as many things from the shelves as they could carry in their baskets.

As a whistle blew, Arthur, Binky and Buster ran down the aisles. Binky headed straight for the sweets!

"I'll take these...ooh, and these...and I'll have some of these!" laughed Binky, cramming his baskets with boxes and bags.

In another aisle of the supermarket, Buster was having a great time in the toy section, filling his baskets with almost every toy and game he could see. He had all sorts of cars, balls and a teddy bear, plus a great new computer game!

Meanwhile, Arthur was being a little more choosy. He put a box of sweets, a bunch of flowers and a teddy bear into his baskets.

"I know who would love this!" grinned Arthur, taking down a brightly coloured beach ball.

The whistle blew for Arthur, Binky and Buster to hurry back to the finishing line.

"Oh, no!" gasped Binky, as boxes and packets fell from his baskets, leaving a trail of sweets on the ground.

Buster wasn't having much luck, either. He couldn't even pick up his heavy baskets! "Gngggg!" groaned Buster, as he tried pushing the baskets along the aisle.

Without any trouble at all, Arthur carried his baskets to the finishing line.

Some way behind, Binky and Buster continued their struggle. But it was no use. As the final whistle blew, they were still a long way from the finishing line.

Surrounded by spilt toys, games and sweets, Buster and Binky looked exhausted as they sat on the ground.

"Remember the story I told you about the greedy monkey?" Mr. Ratburn asked Binky,
Buster and Arthur, a little later.

"Just like the monkey, because we were greedy, we've lost everything!" sighed Buster.

Kind Arthur gave his mum the flowers, D.W. the beach ball and Baby Kate the teddy.
Then he shared his box of sweets with Buster and Binky.

"I'll never be greedy again!" said Buster.

"I've learned my lesson, too!" grinned Binky.

FRUITY WORDSEARCH

E	T	B	A	N	A	N	A	N	A	R
L	A	P	P	L	E	T			A
P	N	O	H	C	A	E	P	S
P	G	R	A	P	E	R	M	P
A	E	A	I	W	I	K	M	B
E	R	E		C	A	E	M	E
N	I	P	O	T	L		U	R
I	N	T		O		O	L	R
P	E	G	N	A	R	O	P	Y

Although he likes sweets, Arthur knows that fruit is good for him. Look at the fruits Arthur has named, then find and circle them in the wordsearch. The names appear up, down, across or diagonally. The letters left over will spell another fruit – which might surprise you!

APPLE PEAR
PINEAPPLE
PEACH KIWI
RASPBERRY
BANANA PLUM
MELON ORANGE
APRICOT
GRAPE
TANGERINE

Turn to page 61 for the solution.

What are They?

Drawn in silhouette are some of the things
that Arthur, Buster and Binky took
from the supermarket shelves.
Rearrange the letters
beneath each silhouette
to spell its name.

Check your answers on page 61.

3

earb edtdy

4

tekiccr tab

2

tewses

1

irormr

5

Ictashe

7 lalb

8 etki

6 etkas

9 eramac

10 aintr

Counting

Arthur and D.W. had a great time cleaning Dad's car! Lots of things in this funny picture are in the shape of a square, circle or triangle. Can you point to them all? Turn to page 61 if you need help.

Sponsored Silence!

Arthur and D.W. were looking forward to going on their summer holiday, but there was just one problem – they didn't have any spending money!

"I'm sure I've got some money in my piggy-bank," said D.W., rushing over to her dressing-table. Holding the piggy-bank in both hands, she gave it a shake. Nothing!

"Shake it again," said Arthur. "I can hear something jangling about inside."

D.W. shook the piggy again even harder. This time, something did fall out.

"Two buttons!" groaned Arthur. "We can't spend those!"

Then Arthur had an idea. Perhaps they could raise some money by doing odd jobs!

"Let's ask Dad if we can wash his car!" said D.W. "That should be worth something."

"I don't see why not," smiled Dad, when the children explained their idea. "But I want my car washed properly. That means using plenty of soapy water!"

While Arthur filled a bucket with water, D.W. fetched two clean cloths.

"You're both doing a very good job," smiled Mum, as Arthur and D.W. washed and scrubbed the car. But Mum soon changed her mind when she saw what the children were using as cleaning cloths!

"My lovely new tea-towels! They're ruined!" gasped Mum, holding up the dirty, greasy cloths, which now had several holes in them.

"Not such a good idea," mumbled D.W., as her mum went into the house, taking the ruined tea-towels with her.

"I think you'd better let me finish washing the car," said Arthur. "I'll use the garden hose and have the job finished in no time."

So, while D.W. went to turn on the garden tap, Arthur held the hose. This was going to be really easy. As water spurted out, Arthur ran backwards and forwards, spraying the car.

"Well done," said Dad, when he saw his car. "You've finished just in time for me to give Grandma Thora a lift to the shops."

But as Grandma Thora opened the passenger door – WHOOOSH! Water poured out and gave her a soaking!

"I guess we should have closed the windows before we washed the car!" gulped Arthur.

"I don't think we'll get paid for this job," whispered D.W. as Grandma went to change out of her wet clothes.

Looking around Arthur's messy bedroom, Mum said, "I'll give you some money if you tidy all this mess away, children."

"Yahoo!" cheered D.W. "Come on, Arthur. What are you waiting for?!"

"Well, now," smiled Mum, when she saw the tidy room. "If I didn't know better, I would think I'd walked into the wrong bedroom!"

Arthur and D.W. felt very proud of themselves as Mum inspected the room.

"No, don't open that door!" cried Arthur.

As Mum opened the toy cupboard, books, toys, clothes and comics tumbled out, almost knocking her off her feet! Arthur had tidied his room by hiding everything inside the cupboard!

"I guess this means we're not going to get paid for this job, either," sighed Arthur.

After having water thrown over her, Grandma Thora didn't feel like shopping after all. Instead, she told Arthur and D.W. that if they bought everything on her shopping list, she would give them some money when they returned.

Taking some bags, Arthur and D.W. ran all the way to the supermarket.

"Even we can't get this wrong," laughed D.W., pushing a shopping trolley around the aisles.

On their way home, Arthur and D.W. met Prunella, who was riding her new bicycle.

"Ooh, can I have a go?" asked Arthur, putting his shopping on the ground.

When he had cycled up and down the pavement a few times, D.W. took a turn.

"We'd better go now," called Arthur, after a while.

A little farther on, Arthur and D.W. almost bumped into Binky as he skateboarded down a slope. Of course, the pair couldn't resist having a ride on the skateboard, too.

Before reaching home, Arthur and D.W. had stopped to play with Prunella, Binky, Buster and Francine.

"We remembered to buy everything on the shopping list," smiled Arthur, as Grandma Thora unpacked the groceries.

When Arthur saw the look on Grandma Thora's face, he knew something was wrong! The ice-cream and butter had melted over the rest of the shopping! Everything was ruined!

"Perhaps we shouldn't have stopped to play with our friends," groaned Arthur, as Grandma Thora took a gooey lettuce from one of the bags.

Our holiday's not going to be as much fun without any spending money, thought Arthur, sitting at the kitchen table in complete silence.

"That's it!" chuckled Dad. "That's how you can raise money!"

"We haven't said anything, Dad," said a confused Arthur.

"Exactly!" smiled Dad. "I will give you and D.W. some money if you promise not to say or do anything for the rest of the day!"

"A sponsored silence!" laughed Grandma Thora. "What do you think of that, children?"

"You mean we won't have to do or say anything?" said Arthur.

"Nothing at all!" grinned Dad. "That way, you might stay out of trouble for a while."

Mum, Dad and Grandma Thora tried not to laugh when Arthur and D.W. held up a hand-written sign which said, 'THANK YOU FOR SPONSORING US!'

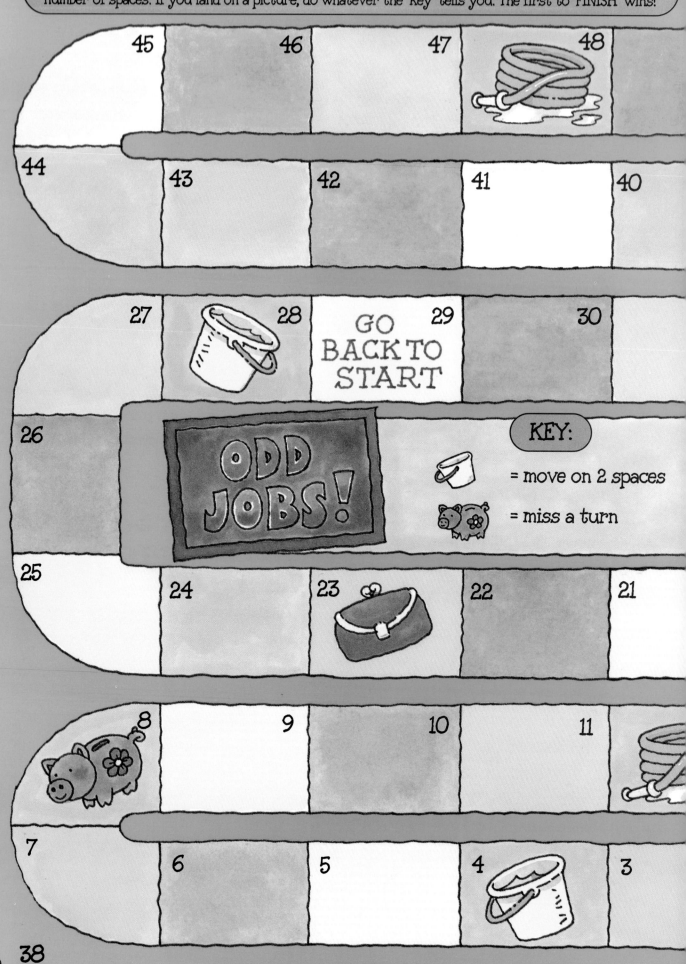

To earn some money, Arthur and D.W. washed Dad's car. To play this game with friends, place different coloured counters on 'START' and take turns to roll the dice. Whichever number you throw, move that number of spaces. If you land on a picture, do whatever the 'key' tells you. The first to 'FINISH' wins!

ODD JOBS!

KEY:

= move on 2 spaces

= miss a turn

GO BACK TO START

38

Secret Message

When Arthur and D.W. tried to raise

He wrote a secret message to his

You can check the message on page 61.

money by holding a sponsored 'silence', clever Arthur had an idea.

sister! To see what the message says, follow the code below.

Following my alphabet code, you can make up your own messages to write to your friends!

Peace and Quiet!

Arthur's dad was quietly reading his newspaper, when Arthur and D.W. rushed into the room, pretending to 'fly' their toy aeroplanes.

"Wheeeee!" laughed Arthur, charging around the sofa.

Trying to find a peaceful place to read, Dad went into the kitchen.

"I'm gonna dance the night awayyy!" sang D.W., dancing past Dad.

Wearing her personal stereo, D.W. couldn't hear how loudly she was singing – but her poor dad could!

Dad tried hiding in Baby Kate's bedroom, but Arthur and D.W. came upstairs, banging and playing their musical instruments!

"Oh, no!" gasped Dad, as Baby Kate woke with a start and began throwing her toys out of her cot.

"Let's all go far away for a short camping break!" said Dad, at last.
"Can Binky come, too?" asked Arthur. "We promise not to be noisy."
"Anything for a quiet life!" joked Dad.

But things didn't go quite as Dad had planned. When Baby Kate wouldn't take her afternoon nap, Binky had an idea.

"Instead of counting sheep, Baby Kate can count these," he grinned, letting some chickens out of a nearby hutch!

As the chickens ran around the field squawking and pecking, Mum and Grandma Thora tried to hide inside their tent.

"Here, chicky-chicken!" called Arthur, chasing after a bird.

After rounding-up the chickens, everyone was exhausted. But then a goat from the nearby farm decided he liked the look of the family's lunch!

"Shoo! Get away!" cried Arthur's mum, as the goat plucked at her jumper.

Arthur and Binky tried shooing the goat to its field, but a 'friendly' cow wanted to join in the fun!

"Run!" called Arthur, as the cow chased them.

SPLAT! Arthur ran straight into Dad, who had been to buy some fresh eggs!

A little later, the goat returned to the camp site.
"Let go, do you hear me?" shouted Grandma Thora, as the goat tried eating her scarf.
"I think he's hungry," gasped Arthur, as he tried to help.
"He's not the only one!" puffed Dad.

Putting a plateful of sandwiches on a table, Mum laughed, "At least the goat hasn't eaten these!"
Suddenly, a swamp of bees appeared!
"Bzzzzz!" went the bees, as everyone, including the goat, raced across a field.

45

Later, when they were sure the bees had gone, everyone returned to their tent.

"Looks like sandwiches are off the menu," groaned Dad, as some ducks pecked at the half-empty plate.

"Waaaa!" wailed Baby Kate, as a duck snatched the biscuit Mum had just given her.

"Waaaa!" shrieked D.W., as a swarm of flies swooped down to eat the sandwich crumbs.

"Oh, for some peace and quiet," groaned Dad.

At last, Arthur's mum, dad and grandma found a peaceful spot.

Back home, while Mum, Dad and Grandma Thora relaxed in the garden, Arthur, D.W. and Binky played around their little tent.

"At least we won't get any cows, goats or chickens chasing after us here!" chuckled Arthur.

But then D.W. looked up and saw a bee...

47

Colour

Before you colour this funny picture, try to find a squirrel, rabbit, bird, hedgehog and mouse hiding somewhere in the scene.

49

First to FINISH!

"Get set...GO!" called Mr. Ratburn, blowing his whistle. Guess who won the race between D.W., Prunella and Francine. Then, following the colour-key, add the seconds together to see if you guessed right.

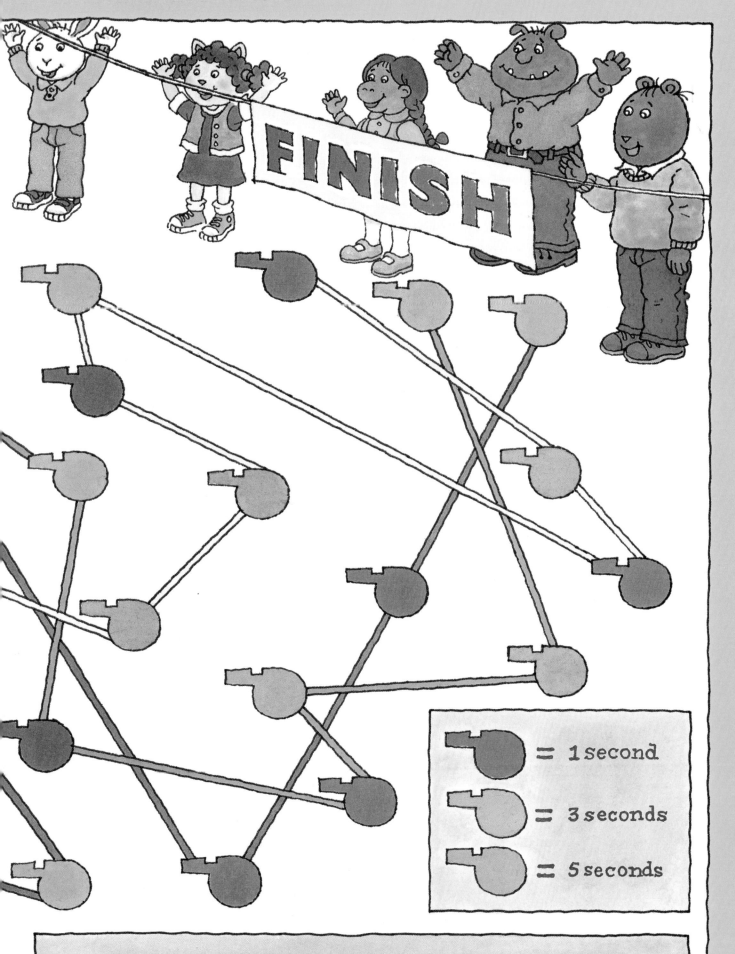

= 1 second

= 3 seconds

= 5 seconds

Turn to page 61 to check your answer.

Keep Fit!

"One, two, three...up! One, two, three...down!" called Mr. Ratburn, as Arthur and his class stretched their arms up into the air, then down to the ground.

"Phew, this is hard," puffed The Brain, as he tried to touch his toes without bending his legs.

"Ten more minutes, then you can all run a few laps around the playground before lunch time," said Mr. Ratburn.

"Run a few laps around the playground!" puffed Arthur. "I don't think I've got enough energy to crawl back to the changing rooms!" Poor Arthur's legs felt like jelly. Several laps of the playground later, and Arthur could barely speak a word.

"W-We need to take up a hobby that w-will help us to keep fit!" groaned Binky, as he and Arthur lay on the ground.

Arthur and his friends
decided to try cycling.
So, early next morning,
Arthur, The Brain, Binky,
Buster, Prunella and
Francine went to the local
park. Climbing on to their
cycles, they pedalled around the
cycling paths.

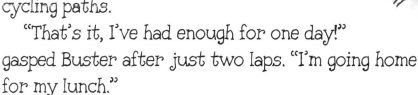

"That's it, I've had enough for one day!"
gasped Buster after just two laps. "I'm going home
for my lunch."

"But it's only nine o'clock in the morning!" said Arthur.

"I know, but all this exercise has made me hungry!" said Buster, rubbing his tummy.

"Well, I'm going to do at least fifty more laps of the circuit," grinned Binky, pedalling
as fast as he could. "Watch how fast I can go!"

Showing off, Binky took a bend too fast, and he tumbled off his cycle! Luckily, Binky only
grazed his knee, but he decided he didn't like cycling any more and wanted to go home.

"We might as well go home too," said Francine, riding away from the park.

"Hey, wait for me!" called Arthur,
climbing back onto his cycle. But his
tyre had a puncture! Instead of
cycling with his friends, poor
Arthur had to push his cycle all the
way home. "This really wasn't the
kind of exercise I had in mind!"
puffed Arthur, pushing his cycle
up a steep slope.

Next morning, Arthur thought
he'd try jogging. But he soon gave
that up as a bad idea when
Grandma, carrying her heavy
shopping, overtook him!

Arthur couldn't believe he could be that slow. Then he realised why he was hardly moving. Arthur had jogged straight into some wet cement! "Oops, sorry!" muttered Arthur, as a workman looked up just in time to see Arthur struggling to pull his feet out of the quick-drying cement.

Back home, as he scrubbed the cement off his trainers, Arthur tried to think of another sport he could do.

Arthur decided to try skipping. But he couldn't quite get the hang of that either.

"I'll teach you how to skip," said D.W., fetching her skipping rope. "Look, copy me. One, two, three...jump! One, two, three...jump!

"Easy-peasy! One, two, three...jump! One, two, three...yeooooow!" spluttered Arthur, stumbling backwards and falling into the garden sand pit.

"Let's play a game of football!" said Francine, bouncing her ball along Arthur's garden path.

Arthur and his friends thought that was a great idea. But playing football wasn't quite as easy as watching it on television.

"Hey, get off me!" gasped The Brain, as Francine tripped and landed on top of him.

Swerving to the left, then the right, Arthur passed Prunella and Binky and raced towards the other end of the field where D.W. stood in goal. "Goal!" he shouted, kicking the ball as hard as he could. But instead of going into goal, the ball hit the goal post, bounced up into the air – and bonked Arthur on the head!

Rubbing his aching shins, Binky said, "Maybe we could play golf. Even we can't hurt ourselves with that game."

But Binky was wrong! Prunella swung her golf club, completely missed the ball – and hit the grass, instead! Too late, D.W. tried to leap out of the way as a clump of earth flew towards her. Then Arthur swung his club, spun round in a circle – and stumbled backwards into a bunker.

With a loud THWACK! Francine hit her ball as hard as she could.

"Good shot!" cheered Prunella, clapping her hands.

But Francine's ball bounced off a tree and landed in the middle of a bramble bush.

"Ouch, owww!" cried Francine, as she tried to find the ball in the big prickly bush!

"Four!" shouted Arthur, finally managing to hit his golf ball. Arthur wasn't sure what 'four' meant, but he had often heard professional golfers say it.

As Arthur's ball sailed through the air, The Brain gasped, "I don't think it's ever going to land!"

But it did! With a loud CRASH! the ball came down – straight through the roof of a greenhouse!

"I think it's time we tried playing another game, don't you?" gulped Arthur.

Before the day was over, Arthur and his friends had played tennis, badminton, netball – and almost every other game they could think of. But every game always seemed to end the same way – in disaster!

"Keeping fit is harder than I thought it would be," sighed Arthur, as he and his friends went home, covered in bruises and scratches.

"I'm beginning to think we could hurt ourselves just playing tiddlywinks!" groaned Prunella. "I ache all over."

When Arthur and D.W. limped into the house, Mum and Dad couldn't help laughing.

"I don't suppose this is the right time to ask how your keep-fit programme is working out!" chuckled Dad, as Arthur and his sister covered themselves with sticking plasters.

"Oh, I'm not giving up yet," said Arthur. "Tomorrow we're going to play cricket!"

"Then remind me to buy some more plasters in the morning!" giggled Mum. "Somehow, I think you and your friends might need them!"

What's Missing?

Can you find six things wrong in this funny picture of Arthur and his friends, as they use the school gym?

Turn to page 61 if you need help finding everything that's gone wrong!

Make a Ball Game

YOU WILL NEED:

large plastic bottles
sticky tape
scissors
paper
string

Trying to keep fit had left Arthur and his friends feeling exhausted, so Arthur made a 'Throw and Catch' ball game they could all play – without too much effort! You can make your own ball game, too!

1. Ask a grown-up to cut down a plastic bottle for you.

2. Scrunch a piece of paper into a small ball, then wind sticky tape round it.

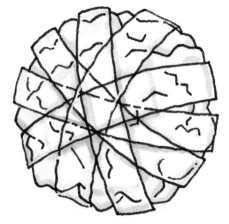

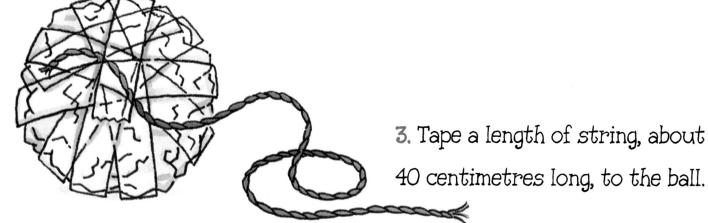

3. Tape a length of string, about 40 centimetres long, to the ball.

58

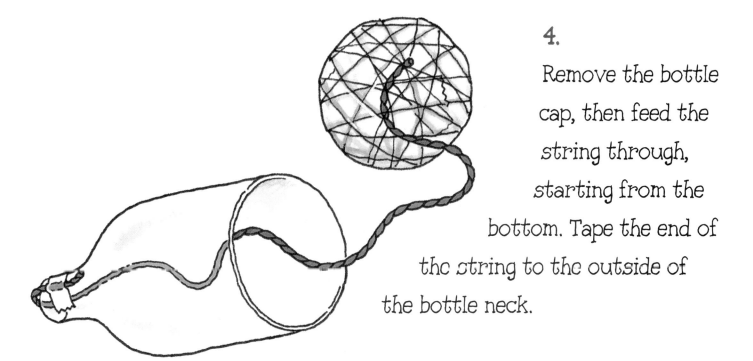

4.

Remove the bottle cap, then feed the string through, starting from the bottom. Tape the end of the string to the outside of the bottle neck.

5.

Just like The Brain and Arthur, rest your ball inside the bottle, then see how many times you can toss it in the air and catch it again!

Puzzle Solutions

Which Path?

(page 13)

Spot the Changes

(page 14)

Hidden Treasures

(page 20)

Slipper - under a bush; Umbrella - on the table;
Glove - in the pond; Pen - in the basket; Spoon
- on the barbeque; Clothes hanger - on the
climbing frame; Sunglasses - on the statue;
Harmonica - on the patio wall; Rollerskate -
on the pergola; Ball - in the basketball net;
Egg - on the pergola; Tambourine - in the shed;
Wool - on the patio; Purse - on the chair;
Cup - hanging from a tree

Matching Sweeties

(page 22)

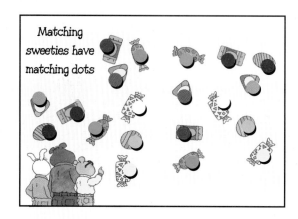

Matching sweeties have matching dots

Fruity Wordsearch

(page 29)

```
E T B A N A N A R
L A P P L E T   A
P N O H C A E P S
P G R A P E R M P
A E A I W I K M B
E   E C A E M E
N I P O T L   R
I N T O   U R
P E G N A R O P Y
```

What are They?

(page 30)

1. mirror	6. skate
2. sweets	7. ball
3. teddy bear	8. kite
4. cricket bat	9. camera
5. satchel	10. train

Shape Counting

(page 32)

Squares: birdhouse, car door handle; sponge
Circles: birdhouse window, car headrest
and wheels, barn window; hose stand
Triangles: birdhouse roof, 4 on barn;
hose stand, hub caps

Secret Message

(page 40)

DEAR
SISTER
I
MISS
SPEAKING
TO
YOU
LOVE
ARTHUR

First to Finish

(page 50)

D.W. took 27 seconds
Prunella took 23 seconds
Francine took 29 seconds

Prunella wins!

What's Missing?

(page 57)

Arthur

D.W.

Baby Kate

Dad

Buster

Puppy Pal